Dear mouse friends,
Welcome to the world of

Geronimo Stilton

The Editorial Staff of
The Rodent's Gazette

1. Linda Thinslice
2. Sweetie Cheesetriangle
3. Ratella Redfur
4. Soya Mousehao
5. Cheesita de la Pampa
6. Mouseanna Mousetti
7. Yale Youngmouse
8. Toni Tinypaw
9. Tina Spicytail
10. Maximilian Mousemower
11. Valerie Vole
12. Trap Stilton
13. Branwen Musclemouse
14. Zeppola Zap
15. Merenguita Gingermouse
16. Ratsy O'Shea
17. Rodentrick Roundrat
18. Teddy von Muffler
19. Thea Stilton
20. Erronea Misprint
21. Pinky Pick
22. Ya-ya O'Cheddar
23. Mousella MacMouser
24. Kreamy O'Cheddar
25. Blasco Tabasco
26. Toffie Sugarsweet
27. Tylerat Truemouse
28. Larry Keys
29. Michael Mouse
30. Geronimo Stilton
31. Benjamin Stilton
32. Briette Finerat
33. Raclette Finerat

Geronimo Stilton
A learned and brainy
mouse; editor of
The Rodent's Gazette

Thea Stilton
Geronimo's sister and
special correspondent at
The Rodent's Gazette

Trap Stilton
An awful joker;
Geronimo's cousin and
owner of the store
Cheap Junk for Less

Benjamin Stilton
A sweet and loving
nine-year-old mouse;
Geronimo's favorite
nephew

Geronimo Stilton

RED PIZZAS FOR A BLUE COUNT

Scholastic Inc.

New York   Toronto   London   Auckland   Sydney
Mexico City   New Delhi   Hong Kong   Buenos Aires

ISBN 0-439-55969-3

Text by Geronimo Stilton
Original cover by Matt Wolf; revised by Larry Keys
Graphics by Merenguita Gingermouse and Marina Bonanni
Special thanks to Kathryn Cristaldi
Cover design by Ursula Albano
Interior layout by Kay Petronio

12 11 10 9 8   6 7 8 9/0

Printed in the U.S.A.   23
First Scholastic printing, May 2004

OH, WHAT A HAIRY, SCARY NIGHT!

Oh, what a hairy, scary night! It was the month of November and it was so cold I had mouse bumps the size of marbles! I buried myself under my great-aunt Ratsy's comforter and opened my book. It was a collection of ghost stories, *The Haunted Cheese Shop and Other Tales to Make You Squeak!* An icy rain pattered against my window as I turned the pages. The wind blew open my window. My curtains danced

Whooosssshhh!

about wildly like a ghost in an aerobics class. I jumped out of my bed to shut the window. **RATS!** I was still shivering, and it wasn't just from the cold. Those ghost curtains looked pretty scary.

As I climbed back into bed, the phone rang. I bounced so high my bed did double duty as a trampoline. **Ring! Ring! Ring!**

Who could be calling so late? It was almost midnight. I picked up the receiver. "Hello, hello! Who is it?" I demanded.

12

Ring!
Ring!
Ring!

"Hellooo? Geronimooo?" a voice answered. It sounded very far away.

"Yes, I am Geronimo. *Geronimo Stilton!*" I shouted.

"It's me, Gerrytails," the voice continued. I groaned. The "me" was my annoying cousin Trap. I should have known. Only Trap would bother a mouse in the middle of the night. Still, he sounded sort of strange.

"Trap, where are you?" I asked. The line crackled loudly. I could only make out some of my cousin's words. But what I heard sent a shiver up my tail.

"I'm . . . in TRANSRATANIA!" he squeaked. "I'm at . . . Castle . . . Count von Ratoff . . . Get out . . ."

Before I could reply, the line went dead. Yes, it was certainly one hairy, scary night!

WITHIN PAW'S REACH

Seconds later, I had my sister, Thea, on the line. "I just had a call from Trap. He may be in trouble," I told her.

"And you woke me up just to tell me that?!" my sister squeaked. "I was in the middle of the most fabumouse dream. I was getting married on an enormouse yacht. Only I couldn't make out who I was marrying."

I wasn't surprised about the last part. My sister has more sweethearts than I have kinds of cheeses in my oversized fridge!

"Listen, Thea," I continued. "Trap said he was calling from Transratania."

"Did you say Trap was calling from TRANSRATANIA?!" Thea cried. "We have to go find him **right away!** Let me check out the train schedule. **We'd better get going!**"

"Wait a minute," I protested. "We can't just go scampering off. What about my job?"

My sister snorted. "Your cousin's in trouble and you're worried about that silly newspaper?"

Oh, yes, I forgot to mention, I run a newspaper called *The Rodent's Gazette*.

"Really, Gerry, your heart must be frozen solid!" Thea shrieked. "*YOU SHOULD BE ASHAMED OF YOURSELF!*"

I chewed my whiskers. "Well, m-m-maybe we could go . . ." I stuttered.

"We'll leave first thing tomorrow morning!" Thea declared. "The train leaves at half-past six! See you at the station!"

WHEN THE CAT
IS AWAY . . .

At six o'clock, I was at the station. I had been listening to the weather report. There would be clear skies all over Mouse Island. But... fog, as always, in Transratania!

Why, why, oh, why did my cousin have to get lost in the coldest part of the island? The coldest and the most mysterious, too. There were lots of stories about the castles of Transratania. Some believed they were stirring with ghosts!

At last, Thea showed up. She was dressed in a smart wool coat with a fake cat-fur scarf and matching hat.

At six o'clock, I was at the station.

"Hey, big brother! How are you?" she greeted me. She was grinning.

"**Awful**, thank you," I grumbled. "How will the paper manage without me?" I worried out loud. "You know what they say: When the cat is away, the mice will play!"

My sister laughed. "Oh, puh-lease, Gerrykins," she scoffed. "You're not all that important. Really!"

"In case you have forgotten, I run a newspaper," I said in my most serious tone.

"If I am not at my desk, who will publish *The Rodent's Gazette*?"

"Oh, give me a break!" Thea snickered. "The office can run just fine without you. In fact, they will probaby be better off. No nervous, old **CHEDDARFACE** breathing down their fur!"

"I am not a cheddarface!" I protested. But I have to admit, I did worry about the paper. After all, mice everywhere were reading it.

"By the way, Gerrytails," Thea interrupted my thoughts. "Do you ever read *The Daily Rat*? I was reading it the other day and—"

Before my sister could continue, I jumped to my paws. "**THE DAILY RAT???**" I squeaked. "How can you read such garbage? You know that paper is written by the slimiest **SEWER** rats in the city! They **would rob** their own mothers for a good story!

Rotten herrings!

They **would feed** a cat the entire graduating class of Mouseville Elementary if it sold papers! That junk is only good for wrapping up rotten herrings!"

"Yes, well, that's all very interesting," Thea said. "But last night, I had a great idea for an article. I will write a story on the castles in Transratania. Horror is very *in* these days, you know." she explained. "Anyway, I've already sold the article. And they paid me a bundle!"

"whattttt did you say?" Why was I so upset? Well, you see, Thea is a special correspondent for my paper, *The Rodent's Gazette*. Could she really be working for my rivals over at *The Daily Rat*?

"whattttt? Are you telling me you want to quit the *Gazette*?" I squeaked. I felt faint.

ON MY RODENT'S HONOR

Just then, I heard a creaking sound. My sister leaped in front of me.

"What's that?" I said. "What are you hiding?"

"Nothing, nothing at all," Thea answered, waving her paw at me. "What would I have to hide? Boy, are you jumpy today!"

I jumped to the left. But Thea was quicker than me. Next, I jumped to the right. Again my sister beat me to the spot.

After a few more jumps, I gave up. "Enough with the dance number!" I shrieked at last. "What are you hiding?"

"Don't get your tail in knots,

Thea Stilton

Gerry Berry," Thea smirked. "It's just a little old trunk."

Benjamin

At that moment, the lid of the trunk opened. A pair of tiny ears popped out. It was Benjamin, my young nephew. "Hello, Uncle Gerry!" he squeaked.

"Benjamin, what are you doing here?" I cried. I turned to Thea. "We cannot take such a young mouse with us to TRANSRATANIA!"

My nephew flicked his tail in the air. "I am not young! I am nine years old!" he insisted. "Besides, Aunt Thea said I could help you!"

That's it, I thought. *For once, I have to show them I'm in charge.* "Forget it!" I announced in my most take-charge voice. "On my rodent's honor, this time we do it my way, or my name is not *Geronimo Stilton!*"

NEXT STOP, RAAATOFF!

Ten minutes later, the three of us were comfortably seated on the train. **Grrr...** *So much for taking charge,* I grumbled to myself. Maybe I shouldn't have dropped out of that Tough-talking Mouse class I had signed up for last summer. The teacher was this old gray rodent with one eye. He had picked on me so much the first day of class, I was afraid to go back!

I sighed and settled back in my seat. My sister was happily reading aloud from a tourist's guide of Transratania. "Hidden in the **foggy** hills of Transratania sits the **MYSTERIOUS** Ratoff Castle . . ."

Meanwhile, Benjamin had snuggled under my coat. "**BRRR, IT'S COLD**, but I don't mind! I'm so happy to be traveling with you, Uncle Geronimo!" he squeaked cheerfully.

I stroked his tiny ears and smiled. Did I tell you that *Benjamin is my favorite nephew?*

An hour later, I pressed my snout against the window. The landscape was getting gloomier and gloomier. At every stop, mice seemed to pour out of the train. But there was no pushing and shoving at our stop. That's because by the time we reached Ratoff, we were the only passengers left!

"Ratoff! Next stop Ratoff!" echoed a lonely voice in the fog.

"Ratoff! Next stop Ratoff!"
"Ratoff! Next stop Ratoff!"
"Ratoff! Next stop Ratoff!"
"Ratoff! Next stop Ratoff!"

GARLIC, GARLIC, AND MORE GARLIC

We climbed off the train and looked around. Now we just had to figure out how to get to Ratoff Castle.

"Excuse me, sir, which way to Ratoff Castle?" I asked a tall, lean rat wearing a ragged coat. His eyes opened wide. He clutched at his garlic necklace. Then he disappeared into the fog without a word.

My sister rolled her eyes. "Let me try," she grumbled. "You are absolutely useless, Germeister!" She tapped the arm of a passing female mouse. "Excuse me, could you direct me to Count Vlad von Ratoff's castle?" she said.

"**Aaaaiii!**" shrieked the mouse. She

Souvenirs from Transratania

scampered off, shaking her bracelet of garlic cloves in the air.

We decided to check out the souvenir shop across from the station. A mouse with a crooked tail stood behind the counter. He looked at us with curiosity.

"Pardon me," I began.

"Ye-es?" said the mouse.

"Could you direct us to a CASTLE?" I continued.

"Ye-es?" said the mouse.

"We're looking for the castle of COUNT VON RATOFF," I finished.

At the name *Ratoff,* the mouse's eyes nearly popped out of his furry face. He flung a handful of souvenir garlic necklaces around his neck. A tag hanging from the necklace read *Greetings from Transratania*. Then in smaller letters it read GARLIC AND ME, PERFECT TOGETHER! How strange. I wondered what it all meant. But I didn't get the chance to ask. Before I knew it, the mouse was shoving us out the door. He clicked the lock behind us and turned out the lights.

"How rude!" squeaked Thea. "What a way to treat tourists! I wouldn't buy his silly souvenirs if they were the last ones in town!" she ranted. "Did you see those ridiculous garlic keychains? And who would want to send a garlic postcard?"

A few minutes later, we passed a fancy restaurant. I read the menu out loud. "Hearty garlic pot pie, jumbo garlic burgers, pasta with extra garlic . . ." What a strange menu!

A large mouse came to the door. "Would you like to have dinner, sir?" he asked. His breath smelled like he had just sampled every dish on the menu.

"No, thank you," I gasped. "But could you tell us how to get to the castle of Count von Ratoff?"

In a flash, the mouse pulled out a **big** bottle and gulped down the liquid inside. Judging by the stench, it must have been garlic juice. "**Get out!**" he shrieked, slamming the door in our snouts.

What was it with the mice of Ratoff and their garlic? I thought about all of the mice we had passed wearing garlic necklaces. I thought about the garlic bracelets and the garlic wreaths on the front doors. *No, this wasn't just a passing trend,* I decided. In fact, there is only one reason why rodents would keep so much garlic. A **SHIVER** ran up my fur. Some say garlic is what you use to keep vampires away. . . .

Who Flew in the Dark of Night?

It was a pitch-black **night**. You couldn't see your nose in front of your snout. We were like the Three Blind Mice trying to figure out which way to run. A sudden flash of lightning filled the black sky.

"That's it!" shouted Benjamin. "That's the castle over there!"

I caught a glimpse of the castle's pointed towers.

"What a perfect picture!" cried Thea happily, pulling out her camera.

Just then, we heard a noise. A very odd-looking steam-powered car rattled toward us. The mouse at the wheel appeared to have a hunched back. He was dressed all in black with a dark hood pulled over his head. The strange rodent was humming an even stranger song.

WHO CROSSED THE SKY IN THE DARK OF NIGHT?

OH, WHAT TERROR, OH, WHAT FRIGHT!

WHO CROSSED THE SKY ON THE WINGS OF A BAT?

DISCOVER THE SECRET, ASK A WISE RAT!

WHO CROSSED THE SKY IN THE DARK OF NIGHT?

OH, WHAT SHEER TERROR, OH, WHAT SHEER FRIGHT!

A large copper boiler was attached to the front of the **funny-looking** car. Pipes of all shapes and sizes stuck out of it. Every now and then, the driver would pull a chain and smoke would shoot out of the largest pipe. The driver would cough and choke.

Afraid of being seen or squished, we dove into the bushes along the side of the road. The mouse drove by, coughing and hacking away. He reminded me of my great-uncle Scratchy before he gave up smoking.

We continued on toward the castle. But half an hour later, we spotted another strange creature. This one wasn't driving a car, though. In fact, it wasn't even on the ground. It was flying through the air. It was black and looked sort of like a

A large copper boiler was attached to the front of the funny-looking car.

gigantic bat.

No, not the kind of bat you'd use to hit a home run out at Ratball Field. I'm talking about the furry black squeaking sort of bat. The kind that comes out at night and sleeps hanging upside down. The strange creature seemed to have come from the castle. It flew over our heads and headed off toward the village.

"W-w-what was that?" stuttered Benjamin as the creature disappeared into the clouds.

"Beats me," said my sister. "But whatever it was, I hope it smiled!" She patted her camera. "I just took its picture!"

ICICLES ON MY WHISKERS

It took three hours to reach the castle. "There are icicles on your whiskers!" my sister told me.

It didn't surprise me. **I WAS SO COLD** I felt like a mouse Popsicle! Benjamin had slipped under my coat to stay warm. I could hear his tiny teeth chattering. We had to find a way into the castle, or we were going to end up in the frozen food aisle at the King Cat Supermarket!

Thea checked out the walls on the side of the castle. I stayed

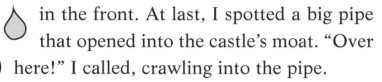
in the front. At last, I spotted a big pipe that opened into the castle's moat. "Over here!" I called, crawling into the pipe.

QUIET AS MICE, we scurried inside. I sniffed the air. "These must be the castle's sewers!" I choked. But there was no time to worry about the stinky smell.

Holding one another's paws, we crept to the end of the tunnel!

REVOLTING, THAT'S WHAT SHE IS!

We dropped into the castle's courtyard. All of a sudden, we heard a doorbell ring.

"**IAMONMYWAYMASTER!**" shouted a voice with a funny accent. It was the rodent we had seen driving that strange car.

"**PHEWIAMCOMINGIAMCOMINGWHAT'S THEHURRY?**" he whined. He hopped down the stairs, four steps at a time. He was **round** and stocky. His head was **sunk** between his shoulders, as if he had no neck. His eyes **BULGED** out of his face. One of his ears was t°rn and looked as if a cat had left teeth marks in it. With one single leap, the hunchback grabbed the key to the front door and turned it in the lock.

"WELCOMEBACKTOTHECASTLE MASTER!" he mumbled, bowing low. The front door opened wide, and in came *an even weirder rodent*. It must have been Count von Ratoff. He was tall and lean, with a pointy snout, and he was wearing a floor-length red silk

cape. His eyes had a sad look and his whiskers drooped, as if he hadn't laughed in centuries. *This mouse needs a night out at a good comedy club,* I said to myself. Stand Up and Squeak! always cheered me up.

Behind him came a little **blonde mouse** who was also wearing a red silk cape. "I hope you remembered to run my hot bath!" she squeaked, staring down her snout at the hunchback.

"**HOTBATH?WHATHOTBATH?**" he answered. He seemed to be trying not to giggle.

"It figures!" she cried. "No one listens to a word I say around here! It's revolting! I don't even have a personal maid! Whoever heard of a countess without a personal maid?!" She swept up the main staircase in a huff. Her silk cape fluttered behind her.

Thea stuck her snout in the air just like the little blonde mouse. "**Revolting**," she whispered. "*That's what she is!*"

GONNNGGG!
GONNNGGG!

We followed the strange mice back into the castle. "Everyone keep their tails low and don't make a squeak," I instructed the others.

"Squeak!" whispered Thea, winking at me. *Why, oh, why will no one ever listen to me?* I thought in despair.

Hiding in the shadows, we crept quietly after the hunchback as he slunk toward the kitchen. A huge soup pot sat on the stove. He stuck a wooden spoon into the pot and tried to stir the contents. The stuff looked as thick as my grouchy grandma Onewhisker's split-cheese soup. You could use that soup to glue down wallpaper!

Eventually, the hunchback's spoon got stuck. "**CREEPYCRAWLYCRABAPPLES!**" shrieked the rodent. He began to pull on the spoon with all his might.

There was a *SUCKING* sound, and out flew the spoon. It hit the wall and stuck there. The hunchback stared at the spoon, then snickered. He bounced over to a huge GONG and hit it with a big hammer.

I peeked into the dining room. The count

and the young countess were sitting at opposite ends of a very long table. The hunchback carried two crystal goblets over to the table. Then he poured a **THICK RED** liquid into each one. **I GULPED**. I had a feeling this was no cherry berry punch. It looked just like blood!

"How yummy!" said the young countess. She wiped her snout with a napkin, leaving **DEEP RED SMUDGES**.

I shivered. The sight of BLOOD makes me *faint*.

POOR TRAP!

"Let's explore the castle while they are having their meal," I whispered.

The long hallways were dark and spooky. Flickering candles cast eerie shadows on the walls. A thick layer of dust and cobwebs covered the furniture and many paintings.

"Poor Uncle Trap! I wonder what's happened to him!" *SOBBED* Benjamin, blowing his nose. He really is such a sweet, sensitive mouse.

Meanwhile, Thea was busy snapping pictures right and left. "**These cobwebs are perfect. Just perfect!**" she squeaked. "I couldn't have asked for a better shot! This is going to be the scariest article ever! I wonder what I should call it? Maybe **BLOOD IN TRANSRATANIA?**" she said thoughtfully. "Or how about **THE CASTLE OF BAD BLOOD?**"

I clutched my stomach. "Please do not mention that word," I whispered.

Thea smirked. "What word, big brother?" she remarked. "You mean, **BLOOD?** As in blood drive, blood sausages, and let's not forget bloodhound?"

I began to turn pale. All of a sudden, a dark shadow loomed in front of us.

TRIP VON TRAPPEN

The ghost of a mouse, white to the tip of his whiskers, appeared before our very eyes. The ghost winked at us. "Hi there, Cousins! Long time no see," he said.

I could hardly believe my eyes. It was Trap! Benjamin threw his paws around his uncle. Even Thea wiped away a tear. **"You're here?"** I gasped. "You're still alive!"

"Alive and kicking, Gerry Doodles! Why, where else would I be? Gone to Mouse Heaven to do a little cloud racing?" my cousin teased. Then he snorted, sending a cloud of white dust into the air. "I was just trying to get a bag of flour down from the shelf, and it spilled all over me. I look like a real bakery mouse, don't I?"

I stared at my cousin. "But, Trap," I said. "What about your phone call? We thought you were in trouble!"

"What phone call?" Trap said. "Oh, yeah, I forgot I called you. You see, I was in the middle of frying up some grasshoppers when I thought I'd give you a call. But then the grasshoppers started hopping all over the kitchen. So I decided to chop up some **HAIRY CATERPILLARS** instead, but they kept inching away. So then I found this **huge fuzzy spider** and—"

Thea flicked her tail at Trap. "**Enough!**" she screeched. "Why did you call, Trap? Do you need

our help? If not, then I need to concentrate on the article I am writing."

My cousin didn't seem to be listening. He had a dreamy expression on his face.

"Well?!" demanded Thea.

Trap snapped to attention. "Yes, well, I just called because I was bored. I didn't mean to get your **whiskers in a knot**. I thought you might like to get out of the city. You know, take a little vacation," he explained. "But now I've met the most beautiful mouse . . ."

I closed my eyes and counted to ten. I was trying not to strangle my cousin. Did I really just leave my job for a little vacation with Trap

Fillet of cockroach!

in Transratania? "But what are you doing here in the first place?"

My cousin cleared his throat. "Are you ready for some **shocking!** news?" he asked. "Did you ever see the commercial on TV for Find Your Tail? You know, that agency that can research your **FURRY TREE?**" he asked.

"Actually, it's **family tree**," I corrected him.

Trap waved his paw in the air. "Whatever," he muttered. "Well, ten days ago, I called the place. And it turns out that I may be a descendant of the distinguished **Von Trappen** family of Transratania! Yes, I may have **ROYAL BLOOD!**" he squeaked.

I groaned. "Don't mention *that* word, pleeeease!" I mumbled. My knees felt weak.

Trap shot me a disgusted look. "Well, it's always been obvious that you and I are very different," he declared. "I am strong, and you are weak. I am carefree, and you are a worrywart. I am an accomplished chef, and you have trouble balancing your cheese on its cracker. Of course, it's not your fault if no royal **BLOOD** runs through your veins," he added.

I practiced my deep-breathing exercises. Why, oh, why did my cousin insist on using **THAT** word?

"Anyway, I came to Transratania to find some proof of my royal beginnings," Trap explained. "They say the *founder* of the family lived right in this very castle centuries ago! His name was **Trip von Trappen!**"

PLEASE, LET ME
FAINT IN PEACE!

"I still don't understand how you convinced Count von Ratoff to let you stay," Thea remarked. "I mean, he doesn't exactly seem like Mr. Friendly Rat."

More like Mr. Frightening, I thought. But I didn't say a word. They would just call me a scaredy mouse.

"Old Ratoff doesn't know about my research," my cousin **chuckled**. "I just got myself hired as a cook. Which reminds me, tomorrow they'll be having a great ball here at the castle. I have to figure out the menu. The count and his niece have unusual tastes. They cannot stand garlic, but they love all kinds of insects! Strange, huh? I don't ask. I just cook. Maybe I should make a nice **BLOODSUCKER'S PIE**, with my hearty **BLOOD SAUSAGE** filling," Trap said thoughtfully. "A creamy **BLOOD PUDDING** would make a tasty dessert. What do you think, Cousin?"

My head was beginning to spin.

"Gee, Gerster, you're looking paler by the minute," Trap said. "You look like you just gave ten pints of **BLOOD** down at the sick mouse clinic."

I closed my eyes. Maybe if I wished really hard, my cousin would disappear into thin air. I opened my eyes. No luck. He was still staring at me as if I were some silly mouse science experiment.

"Ugh! Stop talking about **BLOOD**. Can't

you see it upsets me?" I whispered.

Trap snorted. "Hey, don't blame me if you've got high *BLOOD* pressure. I'm not trying to burst your *BLOOD* vessels. I was just talking about my menu. After all, I'm a *BLUE-BLOODED* mouse now, you know. I don't have time for silly games."

I began to see stars. No, I'm not talking about movie stars. Then **I blacked out.**

Suddenly, my sister was squeaking in my ear. "Geronimo! Take a deep breath!" she screeched, gently slapping my snout.

My cousin leaped to my side and began smacking me hard on the other cheek. My eyes popped open. I glared at Trap. "Please, please, please, just let me faint in peace," I begged.

AH, SNOBELLA . . .

Just then, Trap looked at his watch. "Oh, rats, it's late! I need to get cooking!" he cried. "Count von Ratoff keeps a strict schedule. He's got a timetable for everything . . . eating, drinking, sleeping . . ."

"Flitting around in that creepy cape," Thea added, taking a close-up of some cobwebs.

My cousin smirked. "Maybe you just don't understand us royal mice," he coughed. "Clearly, the count is a noble rodent. And his niece, Countess Snobella, isn't she the most gorgeous mouse you've ever seen?" My cousin sighed dreamily. "Too bad about that fool she's engaged to, *Schnoz von der Nose*," he went on. "He's so ugly he probably cracks every mirror he passes. He's so slow he probably needs his mommy to help him get dressed in the morning. He's so dumb he —"

Before Trap could continue, the bookcase he had been leaning against swiveled around and he disappeared!

"Trap!" we all shouted. But there was no answer.

Seconds later, we heard pawsteps approaching. **We hid behind a large sofa with a crazy zigzag pattern**. I peeked out just in time to see three mice approaching. It was the count, the countess, and the hunchback.

I could hear the countess chattering away. "For tomorrow night's ball, we need a butler and a footman. And, of course, I must have a personal maid!" she squeaked.

Count von Ratoff did not say one word. His eyes stared blankly ahead. This was one depressed mouse.

It was the count, the countess, and the hunchback.

"It's almost dawn. I'd better go. Good night, Uncle!" called Countess Snobella as she headed up a steep, dark staircase.

I watched her glide up the stairs. Very odd. Her paws barely touched the ground. But there was no time to think about the countess. "We need to find out what happened to Trap," I said. "But how can we explore the castle without attracting attention?"

My nephew tugged at my sleeve. "I know! I know, Uncle!" he squeaked. "We'll pretend we are looking for jobs. They are looking for a butler, a footman, and a maid."

"Great idea, little mouse!" I cried. "I will be the butler, you will be the footman, and Thea will be the maid."

"**WHAT?!**" My sister shrieked. "I came here to get a **scoop**, not to play maid to that snobby rat!"

A SCARLET SILK CAPE

We left the castle through the sewers. Then we crept around to the front. It was night, and the castle looked dark and spooky. We knocked at the door. The hunchback greeted us. **"WHATDOYOUWANT?"** he grumbled.

I tried to look very professional. "Are you looking for help by any chance?" I said. "We're looking for work."

The shrimpy mouse smirked and let us in. **"IAMGOINGTOCALLTHEYOUNGCOUNTESS! WAITHEREINTHEHALL!"** he instructed.

A few seconds later, I heard a rustling sound. I turned around, and the young countess was already beside me! *How could she get there so fast?* I wondered. I could tell Thea was just as puzzled as I was by the rodent's speedy entrance.

Meanwhile, Snobella was looking us over carefully. She patted our fur. She checked our teeth. She looked in our ears and waved a paw in front of our eyes. I'm surprised she didn't ask us to walk a straight line or sing a song. Eventually, she seemed satisfied, though, because she waved us on.

"YOU two can go put on your uniforms," she said to Benjamin and me. Then she pointed at Thea. "You can follow me," she told my sister. "You will iron my wrap, sew the hem of my scarlet silk cape, and curl and powder my wig. Then you will polish the

buckles of my silk shoes and . . . well, the list goes on and on. There are just so many things for you to do before the ball!" She gave a smug little wave before scampering off to her room.

My sister shot me a murderous look. I pretended I hadn't seen it. I knew she would never let me hear the end of this one. But I couldn't worry about it now. I quickly followed the sneering hunchback down the dark hallway.

You will iron my wrap, sew the hem of my scarlet silk cape, and curl and powder my wig.

Twelve Strokes

The hunchback led us to a huge walk-in closet. "**YOU WILL FIND YOUR UNIFORMS IN THERE**," he said. "**IF YOU NEED ANYTHING JUST ASK!**"

The hunchback turned to leave. "Thank you," I said, pulling out two matching coats from the closet. "By the way, what is your name?" I called after him.

The hunchback whirled around and squeaked, "**DON'T BOTHER ME!**"

"Oh, well, I didn't mean to pry," I mumbled. "I just wanted to know what we should call you."

"**DON'T BOTHER ME!**" the hunchback cried again.

I gulped. The hunchback seemed to be

getting upset. Maybe he had one of those really embarrassing names. I cleared my throat and tried again. "Lots of mice have names they don't like," I told the hunchback. "Yours can't be that bad."

"**DON'TBOTHERME!MYNAMEISDON'T BOTHERME!**" he repeated.

Benjamin was the first one to catch on. "Oh, of course, Mr. Don't-Bother-Me! That's a great name!" he said.

The hunchback hobbled toward the door in a huff.

"Do you want us to brush off the cobwebs?" I called after him.

Once again, the hunchback whirled on me. "**DON'TYOUDARETOUCHTHECOBWEBS!** he shrieked, going into a tailspin. "**THEY ARESIXTEENTHCENTURY!**"

I looked around the room. "Well, what

about some dusting?" I offered.

Again, the hunchback threw a fit. His tail smacked the floor. He bared his teeth. "**NOOOO!THAT'SCOLLECTORS'DUST!**" he screamed in a rage. "**IWILLCHOPOFFYOUR PAWSIFYOUGOANYWHERENEARIT!**"

"Um, well, what do you want us to do then?" I asked in my nicest voice.

"**GODOWNTOTHEKITCHENANDGIVE THENEWCOOKAPAW!**" the hunchback instructed. He shot a loving glance at the many cobwebs hanging over our heads. Then he stormed off.

Just then, I heard a clock strike. DONG! DONG! DONG!

I counted twelve strokes.

"Midnight!" whispered Benjamin, grabbing my paw. *"Is that when the ghosts and vampires come out?"*

CHERRY RED OR STRAWBERRY RED?

Suddenly, we heard a buzzing noise coming from the highest tower in the castle. It sounded just like an airplane before it takes off. I pressed my ear to the door leading to the tower. The noise got **LOUDER** and **LOUDER**. Then it slowly faded away.

As we made our way to the kitchen, we passed a huge picture window. I glanced outside. Then I blinked. For a minute, I thought I spotted the strange black flying creature we had seen on our way to the castle. I shook my head and peered out the window again. No, nothing there now. Maybe I needed to make an appointment with Dr. Bifocals, my eye doctor, and get my eyes checked. My glasses were sort of old.

At that very moment, we heard voices coming from one of the rooms. I recognized the voice of the young countess Snobella.

"Did you iron my dress? Not yet? Be careful! *CAAAREFUL! YOU'LL BURN IT THAT WAY!*" she commanded.

I heard Thea grumble. Snobella didn't seem to notice. She kept ordering my sister about. "Brush my fur. *Easy, you are tugging at my curls,*" she squeaked. "Now I must have some red polish on my nails, and my whiskers need to be curled." I heard her sigh. "Next, I have to decide which cape to wear. The **cherry red**, the **strawberry red**, or the **tomato red?** What do you think?" she asked. But my sister didn't have a chance to reply. "Oh, what am I thinking?" the countess smirked. "You're just a simple maid. Only *I* can make the right choice!"

Count Schnoz von der Nose

Again I could hear Thea grumbling. This time it was even louder. My sister hates to be pushed around. *Uh-oh,* I thought. *I hope she doesn't get so angry she blows our cover.* Luckily, the countess seemed to have other things on her mind.

"Put these fifty dozen red roses in a vase for me," she instructed. "They're from my fiancé, Count Schnoz von der Nose. Ah, Schnoz," she added softly. "So sweet, yet so boring . . ."

Her voice drifted off. Then I heard the sound of pawsteps. Minutes later, my sister appeared.

"That rodent is a total **nightmare!**" she fumed. "She wants me to help her with everything. I wonder if she even knows how to brush her own teeth! But there is something even stranger about her," Thea continued, lowering her voice. **"She never removes that cape of hers.** I wonder what she is hiding beneath it! She's  probably not a mouse. I think she's really a monster!"

I glanced at Snobella's closed door. "She is very pretty, though," I said with a shy smile.

My nephew joined in. "I think she is one of the prettiest mice I have ever seen!" he cried.

Thea snorted. "She's pretty, all right. Pretty evil!" she snarled.

Just then, Benjamin grabbed my paw. He pointed toward one of the rooms. It had a red door that was slightly ajar. It had to be the count's bedroom.

THE RED DOOR

"Let's check it out," whispered Thea, pulling her camera from her apron pocket. First she took a shot of the hall and the royal portraits hanging on the walls. Then she took a close-up of *Count von Ratoff's* door. It was covered in **dark red velvet**.

"Wait a minute, shouldn't you be ironing Snobella's gown?" I asked my sister.

Thea sniggered. "I'd rather iron her mouth shut," she replied. "Anyway, we need to find Trap. After we do, Ms. Snobby Tail will be ironing her own gown. Of course, she will have to figure out how to turn on the iron first! What a ninny!"

I pushed the door open a little wider. The count's room was a vision in **red**. The deep

red carpet was the same color as the ceiling. Shiny **red** wallpaper covered the walls. Heavy **red** drapes hung over all of the windows.

We approached the four-poster bed. I drew back the **red** satin curtains and jumped. That was odd. There was no mattress! I noticed a strange hook screwed into the wall above where the mattress should have been. I wondered what that was for. Then I spotted a glass containing a pair of dentures. *Count von Ratoff's* teeth were pretty sharp! On the same bedside table sat a crystal glass filled with a **red** liquid. Could it be *BLOOD?*

What is it with these royal rats, I thought. *Do they enjoy seeing a grown mouse cry?* "I am going to **FAINT!**" I realized.

LOOK OVER THERE!

Everything turned black. When I came to, Thea and Benjamin were standing over me.

"Really, Geronimo, you have to stop doing that. You are such a wimp!" my sister scolded.

Benjamin was staring at his new Mega Mouse watch. "It's dawn," he whispered. "The hunchback should be coming back to check on us soon."

Just as he finished talking, the hunchback appeared in front of us. "**EVERYTHING READYFORTHEGUESTSARRIVAL?**"

Thea answered for everyone. "Everything is just perfect!" she squeaked.

The hunchback yawned. "**VERYWELLICAN FINALLYGOTOSLEEPTHEN.TOMORROW**

WEHAVETOGETUPVERYEARLYATFOUR

O'CLOCKINTHEAFTERNOON!" he moaned, slinking off to his bedroom.

Something was definitely wrong with these rodents. Why did they sleep all day and stay up all night? It didn't make sense.

By now, we were all feeling down in the dumps. How would we ever find Trap again? The castle was so large. It could take us weeks just to search one floor!

Benjamin was the first to notice the **red** stain. "L-L-L-Look over there!" he stammered, pointing to a large red puddle on the floor. It seemed to be oozing out from under a closed door. We approached on tiptoe.

"Shhh, no squeaking!" whispered Thea. "This could be ugly."

All of a sudden, the door flew open. My

sister was right, it was ugly. There in the middle of the room stood Trap. He was covered in **BLOOD** from head to toe! The red stain was spreading in wider and wider circles around him.

"Trap!" I shrieked.

He moved a paw, squirting red liquid all over the place. "Oh, hey there, Mouseykins!" he called. "Glad you all decided to hang out. Tonight's menu is going to be to die for!" He turned around, whistling, and took a steaming pot out of the oven. I looked around. We were in the castle's kitchen.

PIRANHABURGERS

"Trap, is everything all right?" asked Thea. Her eyes were as big as fresh balls of mozzarella.

My cousin ran a paw through his fur. "No, no. Everything is all wrong. I am running terribly late!" he groaned. "I still have to peel the **caterpillars**, grill the **scorpions**, and fry the **fleas**. Thank goodness, you guys are here!"

I stared at my cousin's red fur. "But what happened to you?" I cried.

Trap giggled. "Oh, it's nothing. Don't go fainting on me, Germeister," he teased. "A bucket of tomato juice just fell on top of me. Luckily, I've got another one in the refrigerator. So let's see, Cousin, can you cook the **shark** fillets and fry the **piranhaburgers**? **Be careful** with the piranhas. They're super fresh. In fact, they may still be alive!"

I grabbed Trap's paw. "Listen," I said. "We've got to get out of here. You have no idea what we discovered! These *Von Ratoffs* are really **WEIRD**." I told him about how they slept during the day and stayed awake all night. I told him about how they slept in beds with no mattresses. Then I told him about the huge black bat we had seen flying around the castle at night.

SNAP!

SNAP!

SNAP!

"It's all true, Trap," my sister added. "We need to scram now before it's too late!"

Trap just went on cooking without twitching a whisker. "So the rodents are a little out of the ordinary," he said. "**It doesn't bother me**. Besides, I'm not leaving until I've found out about my royal background. I didn't travel all this way for nothing," he insisted. He pulled a cookbook off the shelf and began flipping through it. "Now, what can I make for dessert? How about a nice **dragonfly** pie? That would be nice. I think I saw a crate of fat little **dragonflies** down in the cellar . . ."

Frrrrrrr...

THE SECRET OF A NOBLEMOUSE

Before we could stop him, Trap raced down the stairs leading to the basement. A little wooden door slammed shut behind him.

"**That's it!**" I squeaked. "I've had enough of this! **We're leaving!**" I grabbed Benjamin's paw and headed for the door.

"For once you're right, big brother. Let's go!" my sister agreed. "I've got enough pictures for my story anyway."

SQUEEEEEAK!

Suddenly, a deafening scream made our fur curl. I threw open the door to the cellar. **"Trap! Trap! What happened?"** I squeaked.

My cousin came running up the stairs. He was covered in inky black soot. "I found it, I found it!" he shouted, bouncing up and down like a basketball in the New Mouse City Cross Island Tournament. He danced a jig right there on the steps. Then he pointed to a wooden trunk. The initials on it read *T.V.T.* "Look, I found this trunk right next to a big basket of coal," he whooped.

"*T.V.T.* It has to be *Trip von Trappen's!*"

Hopping up and down with excitement, he opened the trunk and peered inside. He took out a small picture of a chubby mouse with curly whiskers. I had to admit, he did sort of look like my cousin.

Trap dug deeper inside the trunk. "Wow! Look at this!" he cried, pulling out a faded old letter. He cleared his throat and began to read solemnly: "In the year 1605, during the Age of the Rat, under the rule of the Most Excellent, Most Noble, Most Magnificent Grand Duchess Cheesey Lou Linda, the title of Noblemouse is hereby given to Trip von Trappen . . ."

Trap stopped reading. He let out a loud sigh. "Just a *noblemouse?*"

he whined. "I was hoping for something a little more regal. Like a duke or a baron or something."

I chuckled. Trap was so into this royalty stuff. I'm surprised he hadn't started to wear a crown on his head!

My cousin continued reading. "The title of Noblemouse is hereby given to Trip von Trappen, famous throughout the land for his services as a —"

All of sudden, Trap turned as pale as a mouse who just swallowed a whole tray of rat poison. He began to sweat. He rolled up the letter and tucked it into his pocket.

"Wait a minute! You haven't finished reading," Thea pointed out.

My cousin just shook his head. "Never mind, I'll read it to you later," he coughed.

Of course, my sister did not like to be put

off. She leaped to her feet. "What does it say - Trap?" she squeaked. "Put your paws down! Let me see!" She reached for the letter, but my cousin pushed her away. Soon the two were wrestling on the cellar floor. I shook my head. Why did they always have to act like a couple of cranky mouslets? It was so embarrassing! Once I had to pull them apart at my poor Uncle Chester's funeral. My sister had insisted that Uncle Chester had liked her best. Naturally, Trap disagreed, and a fight broke out.

This time, I decided I wasn't going to get involved. Eventually, Thea got her paws on the letter.

"Your forefathers are my forefathers, too!" she cried. Then she read aloud the rest of the letter. "The title of Noblemouse is hereby given to *Trip von Trappen*, famous throughout the land for his services as a

toilet bowl cleaner."

At this point, Trap was sobbing away. "A toilet bowl cleaner!" he choked. "How humiliating! Now I can't tell anyone about my royal background.

What a shame. What a dreadful shame!"

HERE COME THE CARRIAGES!

Just then, the kitchen door flew open. The hunchback came skipping in. **"THEFIRSTGUESTISONHISWAYHERE!"** he announced.

He leaned out of the window to watch one of the carriages approach. **"HOWRUDE NOONEARRIVESEARLYTOABALL!"** he shrieked, running to the door.

I caught my cousin's eye. "Well, what do we do now?" I asked

Trap wiped away his tears. "I must pull myself together and serve dinner," he said, trying to keep a stiff upper snout. *"PLEASE STAY AND HELP ME.* Then we can all leave when the ball is over."

We agreed to stay as long as Trap promised to come home with us after the ball. Minutes later, we heard a shrieking female voice.

"My dress! Where is that foolish maid?!"

it cried. It was Countess Snobella. Thea left, looking rather grim. Benjamin and I hurried off to the ballroom.

The front door opened and the hunchback called out at the top of his lungs, "**THE MARQUISEOFSWEETBLOODANDTHE BARONESSLOWFLIGHT!**"

Meanwhile, more carriages pulled in front of the castle. The hunchback continued announcing each guest. His voice grew hoarse from all the yelling.

"**THEGRANDDUKEOFSILVERWING, PRINCEWOBBLYGLIDE,BARONREDHOT**

BREATH,MARQUISEDEPLASMA,COUNT
SCHNOZVONDERNOSE!"

The guests were all dressed in long silk capes. They glided quietly into the big hall. *Count von Ratoff* welcomed them with his usual sad smile. Rancid rat hairs, he needed some cheering up. Maybe my cousin's insect dinner would do the trick.

MY HERO!

Suddenly, all the guests turned around. Their eyes were glued to a huge winding staircase. At the top stood Countess Snobella. She was dressed in a flaming red ballgown.

I heard someone sigh behind me. It was Trap. He was clutching a big pot of **piranha**

Heeeelp!

soup between his paws. His eyes were glued to the young countess.

Snobella took one small step on the marble staircase. She smiled flirtatiously, then blew a kiss to all her admirers.

"What style! What charm!" Trap whispered, spellbound. Snobella took another step. Then she slipped. She tried to keep her balance, but it was no use. *Thump! Thump! Thump!* The young countess began tumbling down the stairs faster than a gumball in a candy machine!

For an instant, I caught my sister with a satisfied grin on her snout. Did she do something to Snobella's dress to make her trip? There was no time to ask. The next thing I knew, Trap had dropped his pot of soup. **Piranhas** flew everywhere.

"**AHIIIIIIIIIIIIIIIIIIIIIIII!**" I shrieked

as the hot soup rained down on me.

My cousin sprinted forward like an Olympic trackrat at the whistle. "I'LL **SAVE YOU!**" he shouted as he leaped up the staircase.

Schnoz von der Nose, Snobella's fiancé, and a few others tried to follow him. But my cousin was already way ahead of them. He stretched out his paws. Then he caught Snobella in midair.

The young countess looked up at him with an adoring smile. "My **HERO!**" she said with a sigh. ♥ ♥ ♥ ♥ ♥

Trap shrugged. "Oh, it's nothing really," he said, shyly. I could hardly believe my eyes. My cousin was anything but shy.

Then I noticed that poor Schnoz had slunk away into a corner. He sat watching Trap and Snobella, looking very, very sad.

WHO IS HE? WHO COULD HE BE?

The guests couldn't stop whispering about Trap. My cousin ran back to the kitchen to finish cooking. "So much for royalty," he chuckled as he **chopped** up a block of Swiss cheese. "Those stuck-up snouts couldn't keep up with me if they tried!"

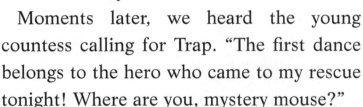

Moments later, we heard the young countess calling for Trap. "The first dance belongs to the hero who came to my rescue tonight! Where are you, mystery mouse?"

In an instant, my cousin leaped to Snobella's side again. "*Countess, I'd be honored,*" he said, taking her paw. The two of them waltzed around the ballroom

"So much for royalty," Trap chuckled as he
chopped up a block of Swiss cheese.

while an orchestra played a romantic song. My cousin held Snobella tightly. She giggled like a young schoolmouse. Around the room, the guests began to gossip. "Who is he? Who could he be?" one rat asked.

"He's a football star," said a second rat.

"No, he's a secret agent," said a third.

Finally, one rodent got it right. "He is the cook!" she squeaked.

Thea was fuming. "That **WITCH**! You males are all such simpletons," she huffed.

Benjamin gazed with respect at the couple whirling across the dance floor. "Uncle Trap is such a good dancer!" he said with a sigh.

"Countess, I'd be honored."

PIZZAS GALORE!

Dong Dong Dong Dong Dong Dong Dong Dong Dong Dong Dong Dong

The clock was chiming. I counted. Twelve chimes. It was already midnight again!

I sniffed the air. What was that awful smell? *Thick smoke* was coming from the kitchen! I waved frantically to my cousin. He got the message, kissed Snobella's paw, and was gone.

"Where did he go? He just disappeared! That rodent is so mysterious!" gossiped the guests.

In the kitchen, my cousin was busy yanking open the oven. Clouds of black smoke filled the room. "Well, this is just great!" Trap shrieked. For some reason, he seemed to be glaring at me. "I should have known I couldn't trust you, Geronimo!" he squeaked. "The **bloodsucker** pie is burned because you didn't get me in time. The **piranha** soup is ruined because you let me drop it on the floor. Even my special dessert is a disaster, thanks to you, Geronimo!" He pointed to a small empty cage. "You even let the **dragonflies** fly away!" he yelled.

I was furious. I was not about to take the blame for this one. I had to stand up for myself. "What are you talking about?" I started. "What has your menu got to do with me?"

But Trap wasn't listening. "Geronimo didn't mess up the whole meal though, right? It can't be that bad," Thea added. I groaned. Why do I always get blamed for everything?

My cousin hopped around the kitchen like a wild rat. "Not so bad!" he squeaked. "Would you like to tell the three hundred and forty-seven guests that they can chew their nails for dinner? I mean, what can I make at this hour? All I have left is some tomato sauce, some **FLOUR**, some olive oil . . ."

Suddenly, Trap's eyes lit up. "I've got it!" he cried. "I'll make a **PIZZA!**"

Benjamin tugged at Trap's sleeve. "But what about the cheese, Uncle?" he asked.

My cousin grinned. **He had a plan.** A plan to make some very unusual pizzas. With the oven fired up, we began cramming in pizza after pizza at breakneck speed. Trap hummed a happy tune as he threw the rounded pizza dough into the air. I must admit, he was pretty good at it.

I decided to go check on the situation in the ballroom. The guests had the hungry look of mice who had been dancing for hours. They drummed the table impatiently with their paws. Their eyes were focused on the door that led to the kitchen. Just then, Trap gave me the signal. I bowed to Count Vlad.

"Dinner is served!" I announced.

At that moment, the door flew open. Benjamin rolled in a cart loaded with pizzas. The guests licked their whiskers.

The pizzas had very special toppings. **There were puréed ants, spicy earthworms, broiled bumblebees, and more!**

"**PIZZAS?**" the guests murmured. "Never tasted one before . . . but these are delicious!"

The meal was a huge success. "Whose idea was it? Who made these wonderful things?" the guests asked. Everyone wanted to know.

*The guests had the hungry look of mice
who had been dancing for hours.*

THE JOKE THAT WORKS EVERY TIME

I was passing out slices of pizza when suddenly I heard a strange noise coming from the kitchen. No, I'm not sure if you could call it noise exactly. It was sort of a mixture of music and noise. I noticed that many of the guests were listening, too. I headed for the kitchen to

bang!

Bang

Bang!

Thump!

thump!

Thump!

investigate. I threw open the door and gasped. The strange sounds were coming from my cousin! Yes, Trap was standing over the sink, drumming on the pots with a big spoon. He turned the tap water on and off with his tail as he hopped about to the BEAT. At the same time, Benjamin was banging on the big garbage can with a broomstick and a large fork.

Just then, the guests began to crowd into the kitchen. "This is where the real party is!" Trap shouted. One rat grabbed a spoon and began banging on a pot. Another rat began to dance. Soon all of the guests were laughing and dancing about the kitchen. It was quite a sight. Thea grabbed her camera and began snapping away.

The only one who did not seem to be having fun was *Count von Ratoff*. He stood off to the side watching the others with a gloomy look in his eyes.

Trap stared at the sad count. "Just watch this! I'll bet I can lift his spirits. No one can resist my jokes," he boasted. "Especially

The Joke That Works Every Time!

He strolled over to *Count von Ratoff*. "Have you heard the latest bat joke?" he said.

Suddenly, the room became **DEADLY QUIET**. All of the guests glared at Trap. He whispered into the count's ear. It was so quiet you could hear a whisker drop.

I held my breath. The count did not move a muscle for a few seconds. Then his fur began to quiver. A strange gurgling noise rose from his throat. It sounded as if he were gargling. He began to roll on the floor, holding his stomach in his paws. He was having a laughing fit! I let out a sigh of relief. We would live! The guests stared, amazed, then they, too, began to giggle.

Ha ha

Trap puffed up his fur. "I told you," he smirked. "It works every time!"

he

le

ho ho hooo!

Ha ha haaa!

93

VON DER NOSE
SCORES AGAIN!

At that moment, the young countess whirled her way through the crowd. She was like a small tornado in a ballgown. "At last, I have found you! What are you doing here in the kitchen?" she asked Trap.

My cousin dropped his spoon and ran to her. "My dear countess!" he squeaked, kissing her paw. "You are the most magnificent mouse I have ever met. **I loved you from the first minute I saw you**. But I am not rich. I am just the cook."

But Snobella did not seem to care. She was staring at Trap as if he were the best thing since sliced cheese!

"Who needs money, my dear Trap," she said.

"Love is all we need to survive."

By my side, I heard Thea snorting. "He's going to need more than love to live with that evil rodent," she grumbled.

I couldn't take my eyes off my cousin. I had never seen him so in love. He seemed so sincere, so sweet. Nothing like the obnoxious pest I knew. Could he really be a changed mouse?

With shining eyes, *Trap bent to give Snobella a hug*. And that's *Hug! Hug! Hug!* when the truth came out. In her excitement, the countess opened her cape wide. Two gigantic, dark wings unfolded in front of our eyes. The countess wasn't a mouse at all. She was a bat!

"**AAAAAAAH!**" Trap cried. My cousin took one look at those wings and fainted. *For once it's not me,* I thought. Then I ran to help him.

Trap came to with a start. The countess stood over him. "Now I understand," my cousin mumbled. "You're a family of bats. That's why you eat bugs!"

Snobella waved her paw. "So what's wrong with a few **mosquitos** now and then? Have you ever tried grilled **grasshoppers?** Don't knock it until you've tried it," she said.

My cousin shook his head. "This is never going to work," he groaned. "We are too different, you and I. I like to travel around, going from adventure to adventure, while you prefer to stay at home in your comfy castle. Plus, for all I know, you probably sleep upside down! And I don't hang out with BLOOD drinkers — and it looks like you drink BLOOD by the gallon!" He pointed to a pitcher filled with a red liquid.

Now the countess was angry. She wrapped her cape around herself and sneered at Trap. "That's tomato juice, you ninny!" she hissed. "And, for your information, sleeping upside down improves your circulation!" With that, Countess Snobella stalked off toward the kitchen door. But before she could leave, Schnoz von der Nose grabbed her by the paw. Then he kissed the bottom of her cape.

"My dear Snobella," he crooned. "Forget that nasty rodent. I'll always love you just the way you are!"

The countess never gave Trap a second glance. She spread her wings and **took off with** Schnoz.

Beside me I heard my sister snickering. "Ah, two bats in love," she sneered. "Isn't it romantic?"

"I'll always love you just the way you are!"

ONE LAST MYSTERY

At last, we knew the real story behind *Count von Ratoff* and his niece. Bats do not walk. Bats use their wings to fly. That is why the count and young countess appeared and disappeared so quickly. Bats do not sleep on mattresses. They sleep upside down. The count must have used the hook in his room to do just that. Bats do not eat cheese. They eat all kinds of bugs. That would explain the rodents' **STRANGE EATING HABITS**.

But there was still one more mystery left to solve. What was that strange NOISE coming from the highest tower of the castle? Being a newspaper mouse, I just had to find out the real story. Luckily, I didn't have to wait long to get the scoop.

The strange noise started up again at that very moment.

I raced up to the tower. There, under the moonlight, stood the hunchback. He was putting on a pair of very old-fashioned flying goggles. Then he climbed into a huge black plane with wings shaped like a bat. *Count von Ratoff* was waiting on board, grinning. The hunchback turned around and waved his paw at me.

"**HOWDOYOULIKEOURPLANE? WE BUILTITBECAUSECOUNTVONRATOFF SUFFERSFROMARTHRITISANDCANNOT FLYLONGDISTANCESANYMORE,**" he shouted in the wind. Then the plane took off.

No wonder the rodents down in the

village had so much garlic. The count's plane looked just like an enormous vampire bat!

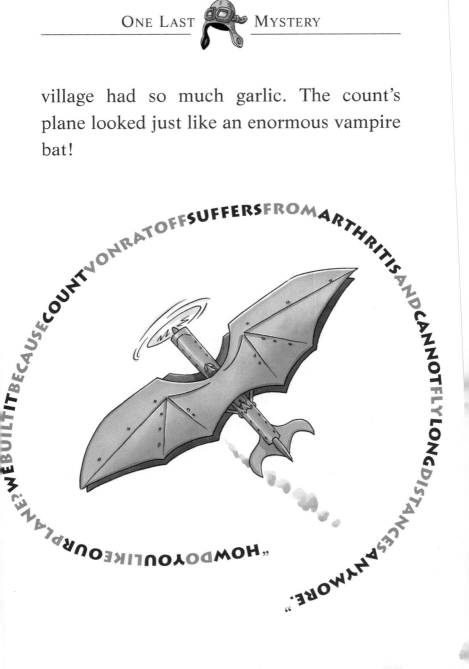

"HOW DO YOU LIKE OUR PLANE? WE BUILT IT BECAUSE COUNT VON RATOFF SUFFERS FROM ARTHRITIS AND CANNOT FLY LONG DISTANCES ANYMORE."

THE SADDEST STORY
EVER TOLD

I went back downstairs to the dining room. Leftover pizzas littered the table. Red tomato juice dripped down the chairs. An enormous vase of black roses had crashed into a million pieces onto the floor. What a rats' nest!

We all pitched in and cleaned up. By the time we had finished, it was almost dawn. The guests had all left. Except for one. We found him hanging upside down in a closet, fast asleep.

"This is going to be a first-rat story," Thea squeaked, taking a quick picture of the snoring guest. "The pictures of the ball are going to be *PHENOMENAL!*"

I checked my watch. "There is a train

leaving at seven," I said. "Are we all ready to go?"

Benjamin nodded his head. "I guess so, Uncle," he said with a sigh. "But I was beginning to like the castle. These cobwebs are kind of neat."

I smiled. Only my sensitive little nephew could fall in love with cobwebs.

We headed down the long hall. As we passed the count's red door, we heard a strange noise. It was someone laughing. The door flew open, and there was *Count von Ratoff*. He was sprawled on a chair in a fit of giggles.

I turned to Trap. "Crumbling cheese bits! He's still laughing at your joke,"

Hee, hee, hee! Ha, ha, ha! Hee, hee, hee! Ha, ha, ha! Hee, hee, hee! Ha, ha, ha! Hee, hee, hee!

I croaked. "Can you make him stop? He's laughing so hard he's going to bust a wing!"

Trap scratched his head with his paw. "Yes, I recognize the symptoms. **The Joke That Works Every Time** can have a big effect on certain rodents. Stand back. I will handle this."

He walked over to the count and mumbled something in his ear. My cousin must have been telling the count his whole life story. Finally, he stopped. All at once, *Count von Ratoff* stopped laughing. Then he began crying. No, I'm not talking little tiny boo-hoo tears. He looked like a waterfall wearing a cape. If he cried any harder, we'd have to swim home!

"What did you do to him?" Thea shrieked.

Trap just winked. "Don't worry. I just told him **THE SADDEST STORY EVER TOLD**. It never fails. He'll cry for half an hour, and then it'll all be over!"

We waved good-bye to the count. Then we headed for the main entrance and out the front door. The hunchback stood on the steps, waving a big handkerchief. "**GOOD-BYE, COME BACK SOON! IT HAS BEEN A PLEASURE HAVING YOU HERE!**"

My mouth dropped open. The hunchback's words were not blended together. He could speak perfectly clearly. He must have been pulling our paws the whole time!

I quickly turned back to say farewell. But he had already disappeared in the thick Transratanian fog.

NEXT STOP, NEW MOUSE CITY!

Our trip back to New Mouse City seemed even longer than the trip out. Thea was in a great mood. She pulled out her laptop computer and began typing up her article on the Transratanian castles. For once, Trap was not chattering away. He just stared out the window with a sad smile. I had a feeling he was still thinking about Snobella. Benjamin had fallen asleep in my lap, wrapped in my scarf.

I watched the fog roll by as the train chugged along. I couldn't wait to get back home. *No more traveling for this mouse*, I promised myself. Not for years to come!

THE FURRY TREE

When I got home, I fell into my comfy bed.

At midnight, I woke up with a jolt. Someone was ringing my doorbell. I pulled on my bathrobe and shuffled to the door. "Who is it?" I mumbled.

"I am an evil spirit!" called out a shaky voice.

I gulped. Could it really be a ghost? Could one have followed me all the way home? I looked through the peephole. No, there was not a ghost outside my door. It was only Trap.

"Did I scare you?" he sniggered.

I banged open the door. "What do you want?" I squeaked, annoyed.

My cousin brushed by me. "Have you heard the news?" he said. "The agency made a mistake. I am not a descendant of the *Von Trappens*. But I may be related to Maximilian of Mousehara. Look, I've got the *furry tree*!"

"It's a *family tree*, not a furry tree," I sighed.

Trap wasn't listening. "It turns out my ancestor was a famous explorer. He traveled to the far corners of the Mousehara Desert," he babbled on. "I'm going there myself. To Mousehara, I mean. You're going to come with me, right? By the way, since my forefathers are yours, too, I told the agency to bill you for the whatchamacallit, you know . . . the furry tree."

Before he could say another word, I leaped across the room and threw him out the door, screaming, "Get lost!"

It felt as if I had been away for a whole month.

BACK AT MY DESK

Next morning, I was back at my desk. Phone calls, faxes, e-mail . . . it felt as if I had been away for a whole month, not for just a few days!

My sister flew into my office like a tornado. "**Take a look at this!**" she shrieked, throwing a bunch of photos on my desk. "You can see the castle, the staircase, the courtyard, even the cobwebs. But I do not have one picture of any of the guests!" she squeaked. "I wonder how those rotten bats did it?!"

I picked up my magnifying glass. Then I examined each picture. "You're right," I agreed. "The castle looks deserted."

Thea stamped her paws. "I cannot believe

this! Now I have to give back the money I got from *The Daily Rat* for my story!" she grumbled.

I tried not to laugh out loud. *Serves her right for trying to work for the slimy* Daily Rat, I thought.

"Maybe the legend about the ghosts living in that castle really is true after all," I said.

My sister just rolled her eyes. "Oh, Geronimo," she smirked. "You're so gullible." Then she placed her elbows on my desk. "By the way, have I ever told you about Mousehara?" she whispered.

MOUSEHARA, MOUSEHARA, MOUSEHARA!

I sat up straight. Uh-oh. This was the second time I had heard the word *Mousehara*. Something told me my sister had been talking to Trap. "What about Mousehara?" I asked cautiously.

Just as I thought. My sister had been talking to my cousin. She told me about the great idea he had. She could do a special report on the secrets of the Mousehara Desert. She could do an interview with the chief of the Mousareg, mysterious *blue rats* who lived there. "I can just see the headline already! *Mousehara, Mousehara,*

Mousehara!" Thea squeaked. "Oh, and of course you'd have to come with me," she added.

I put my head in my paws. *"THIS IS NOT HAPPENING,"* I groaned. "First, you drag me off to Transratania, the coldest place on the island, with fog thicker than cream cheese, and now . . ." I stopped to catch my breath.

Splaatt!

"And now you want me to go to the Mousehara? Do you know it is the hottest place on the island? The temperatures reach 120 degrees in the shade! You can fry an egg on top of a rodent's head there!"

Hottt!

My sister twirled her whiskers. "Gerry, dear,

THE RODENT'S GAZETTE

DOSSIER
Truths and lies
about the blue rats!

HEALTH
How to survive in 120°
Fahrenheit in the
shade.

COOKING
Eat with the Mousareg!
Exotic recipes with
spicy cheese.

**The blue rats
reveal all!**
From our special
reporter,
Thea Stilton

VACATION
Sun, sand,
and palms in
the oases of
Mousehara.

ADVENTURE
The Mousehara
Trophy.

**"STUNG BY A HUMONGOUS SCORPION,
AND I AM STILL HERE TO TELL THE TALE!"**
says the chief of the Mousareg!

you are such a whiner," she said. "Now, if you come with me I will sell my story to you. Otherwise I will offer it to *The Daily Rat*. You have five minutes to make up your mind," she added, drifting out of the office.

After she left, I stared at my watch. It only took me two minutes to make up my mind. My sister can be a real pain, but she can smell a scoop a mile away! I could already see the headlines in *The Rodent's Gazette*. . . .

Want to read my next adventure?
It's sure to be a fur-raising experience!

ATTACK OF THE BANDIT CATS

Captured by cats! It's every rodent's worst nightmare. It all started when my cousin Trap convinced me to join him on a quest for a legendary island covered in silver. We set out by hot-air balloon. But before you could say "hot cheese on toast," we were attacked by a ship of pirate cats! They mousenapped us and threatened to cook us for dinner. Would we escape with our lives . . . or end up in the soup?

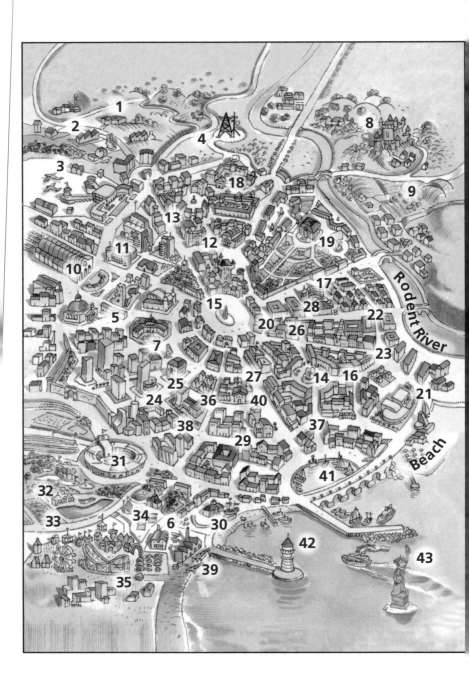

Map of New Mouse City

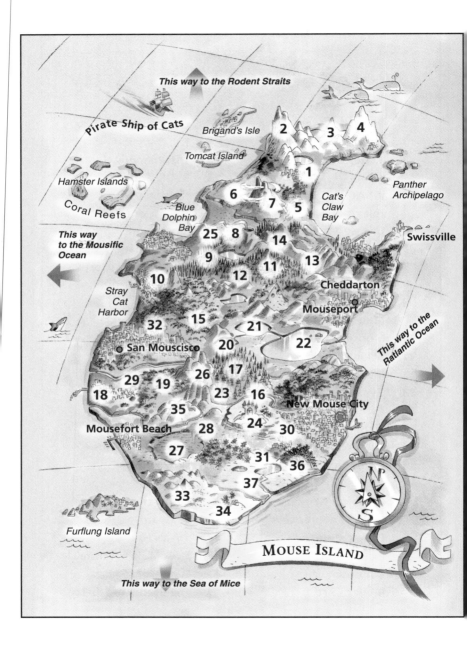

Map of Mouse Island

1. Big Ice Lake
2. Frozen Fur Peak
3. Slipperyslopes Glacier
4. Coldcreeps Peak
5. Ratzikistan
6. Transratania
7. Mount Vamp
8. Roastedrat Volcano
9. Brimstone Lake
10. Poopedcat Pass
11. Stinko Peak
12. Dark Forest
13. Vain Vampires Valley
14. Goose Bumps Gorge
15. The Shadow Line Pass
16. Penny Pincher Lodge
17. Nature Reserve Park
18. Las Ratayas Marinas
19. Fossil Forest
20. Lake Lake
21. Lake Lake Lake
22. Lake Lakelakelake
23. Cheddar Crag
24. Cannycat Castle
25. Valley of the Giant Sequoia
26. Cheddar Springs
27. Sulfurous Swamp
28. Old Reliable Geyser
29. Vole Vail
30. Ravingrat Ravine
31. Gnat Marshes
32. Munster Highlands
33. Mousehara Desert
34. Oasis of the Sweaty Camel
35. Cabbagehead Hill
36. Tropical Jungle
37. Rio Mosquito

Dear mouse friends,
thanks for reading, and farewell
till the next book.
It'll be another whisker-licking-good
adventure, and that's a promise!

Geronimo Stilton